the Littlest Dragon

ROARING GOOD READS

Collins

Roaring Good Reads will fire the imagination of all
young readers – from short stories for children just
starting to read on their own, to first chapter books and
short novels for confident readers.
www.roaringgoodreads.co.uk

Also by Margaret Ryan

The Littlest Dragon Gets the Giggles
The Littlest Dragon Goes for Goal
The Littlest Dragon at School

More Roaring Good Reads from Collins

Morris and the Cat Flap *by Vivian French*
Spider McDrew *by Alan Durant*
Daisy May *by Jean Ure*
Mister Skip *by Michael Morpurgo*

the Littlest Dragon

MARGARET RYAN

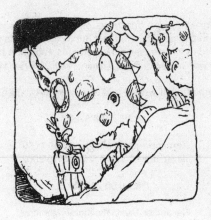

Illustrations by Jamie Smith

ROARING GOOD READS

Collins

An imprint of HarperCollinsPublishers

First published in Great Britain by CollinsChildren'sBooks in 1996
This edition published in Great Britain by Collins in 2002
Collins is an imprint of HarperCollins*Publishers* Ltd
77-85 Fulham Palace Road, Hammersmith, London W6 8JB

The HarperCollins website address is www.**fire**and**water**.com

1 3 5 7 9 8 6 4 2

Text copyright © Margaret Ryan 1996
Illustrations © Jamie Smith 1996/2002

ISBN 0 00 767521 6

The author asserts the moral right to be
identified as the author of the work.

Printed and bound in England by Bookmarque Ltd, Croydon

Contents

The Littlest Dragon   7

The Littlest Dragon and the
Special Game of Football   44

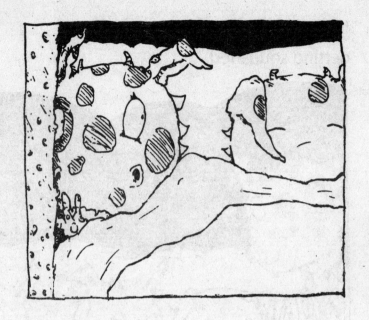

The Littlest Dragon

It was deep dark night-time.
In the dragons' cave, ten dragons lay
in the big dragons' bed. Nine of the
dragons were snoring, but the littlest
one, Number Ten, wasn't. He lay on his
side with his nose jammed up against
the cave wall.

He couldn't sleep because he was
getting squashed.

"Move over, Number One," he
shouted to his biggest dragon brother
on the other side of the bed.

"Snnnnnorrrrre, snnnnorrrre, snnnnorrrrk," said Number One.

"Shove along a bit, Five and Six," he called to his middle-sized brothers who were twins.

9

"Eeeeee wheeeee whistle," said
Numbers Five and Six.

"You've got your right elbow in my
ear," he said to Number Nine, who was
asleep beside him.

"Three blind mice," said Number Nine, who always chanted nursery rhymes in his sleep.

"This won't do at all," said the littlest dragon. "I'll never get to sleep at this rate."

He wriggled as best he could, and squiggled as best he could. But it was no use.

He was sandwiched between the
cave wall and his sleeping brothers.
Then, he had his first idea.

"Breakfast time, boys," he called in a high voice, very like his mum's.

The big bed shook as nine dragons leapt out of it and headed for the door, shouting…

"Oh goody, I'm starving…"

"I want toast soldiers…"

"I could eat two basins of porridge…"

"Me too…"

"Let go of my tail…"

"I was first."

The littlest dragon gave a smile and a sigh and snuggled down in the big warm bed.

At last he had the bed to himself.

But not for long. Soon the other nine dragons were back.

"It's not breakfast time at all," said Number Eight.

"It's the middle of the night," said
Number Four.

"We were sure we heard Mum's
voice calling us," said Numbers Five
and Six.

"Zzzzzzzzz," said the littlest dragon. But that soon changed to "Owwwwwww," as all the other dragons piled back into the big bed and squashed his nose back up against the wall.

The littlest dragon rubbed his nose
and had a serious think. After a few
moments, he had his second idea.

He waited till the other dragons were
fast asleep and he could count all the
different snores.

"Snnnnnorrrrre, snnnnorrrre, snnnnorrrrk," went Number One.

"Snnnnnuffffle, snnnnnnuffffle, snniffff," went Number Two.

"Urrk, urrk, oink," went Number Three.

"Burrrrble, burrrrble, boink," went Number Four.

"Eeee, wheeeee, whistle," went
Numbers Five and Six.

"Baaaaa, baaaa, baaaaa," went
Number Seven, who still counted sheep
in his sleep.

"Aaaaaarrrrooooooaaaaarrrr," went
Number Eight.

"Tom, Tom the piper's son," said
Number Nine.

"Right," said the littlest dragon. He
called in a deep voice very like his dad's,
"Time for a game of football, boys."

The big bed shook as nine dragons leapt out of it and headed for the door, shouting, "That's my football jersey, give it back…"

"I can only find two left boots…"

"My lace is broken…"

"No cheating like last time…"

"Whose smelly socks are these…?"

"Last outside's a dozy dragon…"

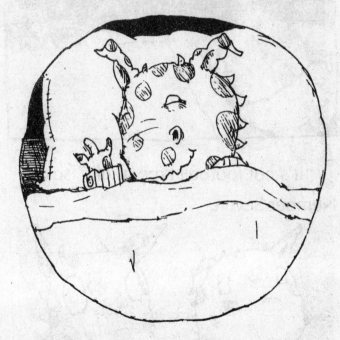

The littlest dragon gave a smile and a sigh and snuggled down in the big warm bed.

At last he had the bed to himself. But not for long. Soon the other nine dragons were back.

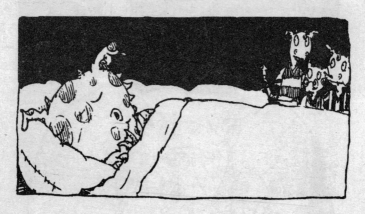

"It's not football time at all," said Number Seven.

"It's still the middle of the night,"
said Number Three.

"I was sure I heard Dad's voice
calling us," said Number Two.

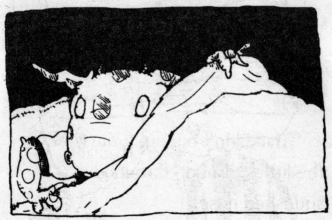

"Zzzzzzzz," said the littlest dragon, but that soon changed to "Owwwww," as the dragons piled back into the bed and squashed his nose back against the wall.

"Thidz idn't bunny," muttered the littlest dragon through his squashed nose.

Then he had his third idea. If he
couldn't get to sleep lying beside his
brothers, perhaps he could get to sleep
lying on top of them.

So he clambered up and lay on
brothers Nine, Eight and Seven.

"Get off, Number Ten, and let us get
some sleep," they all said and bounced
him up in the air.

When he came down, he landed on brothers Six, Five and Four.

"Get off, Number Ten, and don't be such a pest," they all said and bounced him up even higher in the air.

When he came down, he landed on brothers Three, Two and One.

"Get off, Number Ten. Get back to your own space," they all said and bounced him up so high into the air that he didn't come down again, but landed on a broad ledge near the roof of the cave.

"Oh dear," said the littlest dragon, peering down into the dimly-lit cave. "How am I going to get down from here?"

Then he had his fourth and best idea.

"Oh, how nice it is up here," he said
in a squeaky voice. "What a cosy place
to sleep. And all to myself too. How nice
it is to have a place of my own at last."

"A place of his own?" said the other nine dragons. "We'll soon see about that." The big bed shook as they all leapt out, got themselves a long ladder and climbed up to join Number Ten.

"It is nice up here," said brothers One, Two and Three, elbowing the littlest dragon out of the way.

"Very cosy," said brothers Four, Five and Six, nudging the littlest dragon over a bit more.

"He can't possibly have it all to himself," said brothers Seven, Eight and Nine. "What about the rest of us?"

"You're quite right," said the littlest dragon hurrying down the long ladder, and pulling it away. "You have it all to yourselves instead."

"Come back with that ladder this minute, Number Ten," shouted the other dragons. "We can't all sleep up here. We'll be squashed."

But the littlest dragon wasn't listening.
He had already climbed back into the
big warm dragons' bed. With a smile
and a sigh, he snuggled down and
went to sleep.

"Zzzzzzzzzzz…"

The Littlest Dragon and the Special Game of Football

It was a bright sunny afternoon.
In the dragons' cave, the ten dragon
brothers were getting ready to go to
the next field to watch their favourite
football star, Dragon McFeet, play a
special game.

"I've got to get properly dressed to go to the match," said the littlest dragon.

He went to the big chest in the dragons' cave and put on the best football jersey he could find, the best football shorts he could find and the best football socks and boots he could find.

Then he looked at himself in the
big mirror.

"What a handsome looking
dragon," he said.

At that moment, big dragon brother
Number Nine appeared.

"Oi, Number Ten," he said, "that's
MY football jersey you've got on.

I'm wearing that to the game. Get it off this minute."

"OK," sighed the littlest dragon, "but can I borrow it when you're not using it?"

"I'll think about it," said Number Nine.

Then big dragon brother, Number Eight, appeared.

"Oi, Number Ten," he said, "those are MY football shorts you've got on. I'm wearing them to the game. Get them off this minute."

"OK," sighed Number Ten, "but can I borrow them when you're not using them?"

"I'll think about it," said Number Eight.

After that, twin dragon brothers Numbers Five and Six appeared.

"Oi, Number Ten," they said, those are OUR football socks and boots you've got on. We're wearing them to the game. Get them off this minute."

"OK," sighed Number Ten, "but can I borrow them when you're not using them?"

"We'll think about it," said Numbers Five and Six.

Then all the dragon brothers went off to the game leaving the littlest dragon standing there, in his pink stripy underpants, all alone.

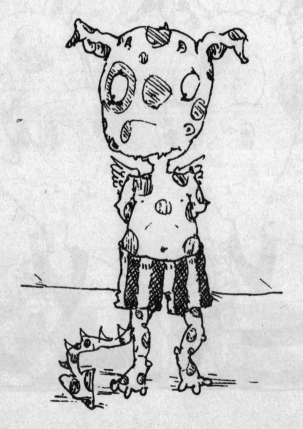

"It's not fair," he muttered, stomping into the big cave kitchen. "I always get left out, just because I'm the littlest."

"What's not fair, Number Ten?" asked his mum, who was baking special football cookies for the dragons' tea.

"It's not fair that they all get to go to the special football game to see Dragon McFeet and I don't. Just because I don't have a proper football strip."

"You don't need a proper football strip to WATCH the game," said his mum. "Why don't you try out some of these special football cookies instead, to see if they're all right."

The littlest dragon tried some football cookies. They tasted delicious, but he tried some more anyway, just to be sure.

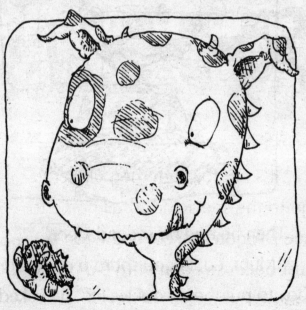

Then he had his first idea.

"Mum, could you spare some of these football cookies for a friend?" he asked.

"Certainly," said his mum and gave him some.

Then he had his second idea.

"Mum, could you spare a cardboard box to put these cookies in?" he asked.

"Certainly," said his mum and gave him one.

Then he had his third idea.

"Mum, could you spare a big piece of paper I could draw on?" he asked.

"Certainly," said his mum and gave him a big piece of paper.

Then his mum had an idea.

"Number Ten, could you spare a minute to go and put some clothes on before you catch cold?" she said.

"Certainly," said the littlest dragon, and went and put on his tracksuit.

Then he started work on the big piece of paper with his coloured crayons. He drew careful lines all over it and coloured in between them very neatly. It took him ages.

When he was finished, he put the football cookies into the cardboard box, wrapped the box up in the coloured paper, and tied it carefully with some string he'd found in his tracksuit pocket.

"I'm just off to give these cookies to a friend, Mum," he called, and set off for the special football game in the next field.

When he got there, the game was in full swing. He could see his brothers just behind the nearest goal, and they were grinning from ear to ear. "We're winning," they told him. "Dragon McFeet has scored three goals already."

"Good," said the littlest dragon and
settled down to watch the rest of the
game. He saw Dragon McFeet score
three more goals before the game
was finished.

Then the players came off the field right past the dragon brothers.

"Brilliant, wonderful, superb play, Dragon McFeet," shouted dragon brother Number Nine.

Dragon McFeet smiled and waved.

"Six beautifully placed goals, Dragon McFeet," called dragon brother Number Eight.

Dragon McFeet smiled and waved.

"Fantastically fast footwork," chorused twin dragon brothers Five and Six.

Dragon McFeet smiled and waved.

Then the littlest dragon stepped forward and handed Dragon McFeet the box of special football cookies.

"I brought you these cookies because I think you're the very best player in the whole of Dragonland," he said.

"Well, thank you very much, Littlest Dragon," said Dragon McFeet. "What a kind thought. And look, the stripes on the paper are the same colours as those on my jersey. Did you colour them in all by yourself?"

"I did," said the littlest dragon.

"And did you manage to tie this nice bow all by yourself?"

"I did," said the littlest dragon.

"And did you manage to make the football cookies all by yourself?"

"I didn't," said the littlest dragon.

"My mum made them, but I tasted them for you. They're delicious."

"Well," smiled Dragon McFeet. "I think that deserves a little reward." And he took off his special winning jersey and gave it to the littlest dragon.

"Oh, THANK YOU, Dragon McFeet,"
said the littlest dragon. He wore the
winning jersey, which came right down
to his toes, all the way home.

Next day the dragon brothers went out
to play their usual game of football.

"You can borrow my football
jersey if you like, Number Ten," said
Number Nine.

"Thank you," said the littlest dragon and put it on.

"You can borrow my football shorts if you like, Number Ten," said Number Eight.

"Thank you," said the littlest dragon and put them on.

"You can borrow our football socks and boots if you like, Number Ten," said twin dragon brothers Five and Six.

"Thank you," said the littlest dragon and put them on.

"And you can borrow any of our football things, any time you like," said all the other dragon brothers.

"Thank you," said the littlest dragon, "and I suppose you all want to borrow Dragon McFeet's special winning jersey when I'm not using it."

"Can we? Can we?" said the brothers.

"I'll think about it," said the littlest dragon.

Order Form

To order direct from the publishers, just make a list of the titles you want and fill in the form below:

Name ....

Address ....

....

....

Send to: Dept 6, HarperCollins Publishers Ltd, Westerhill Road, Bishopbriggs, Glasgow G64 2QT.

Please enclose a cheque or postal order to the value of the cover price, plus:

UK & BFPO: Add £1.00 for the first book, and 25p per copy for each additional book ordered.

Overseas and Eire: Add £2.95 service charge. Books will be sent by surface mail but quotes for airmail despatch will be given on request.

A 24-hour telephone ordering service is available to holders of Visa, MasterCard, Amex or Switch cards on 0141- 772 2281.

Collins

An imprint of HarperCollins*Publishers*